The day the custodian found the bad-something on the bathroom wall, all the girls from Mr. Gilbert's class were called into the principal's office.

The principal asked if we had any information.

Some girls said, "No, Mrs. Martínez."

Some girls stared down at the carpet.

Mrs. Martínez took her time looking at each of us.

She seemed very serious and very sad.

She said quietly but firmly, "This kind of thing won't be tolerated at our school."

We all started fidgeting. We wanted to know: *What is the bad-something? Who did it? And what will happen next?*

The principal said no one was allowed to use that bathroom, but after lunch, Kiyoko made a run for it, and me and Tanisha and Emmie were right behind her. We giggled our way in and shut the door, then shushed each other as we looked around, and over, and on, and under.

Until we saw it.

The bad–something.

My mouth popped open. Tanisha turned around and ran out. Kiyoko kicked a stall really hard, and the sound made us cover our ears. Emmie started to cry.

The next day, that bathroom door was locked. The girls had to go all the way up to the second floor.

Why do the boys have it easy? us girls thought.
How does the principal even know it was a girl
who did it? A boy could have snuck in.

We all watched our classmates. We studied their faces to see if anyone looked guilty. We tried to remember who had gone to the bathroom and when, but most of all we wanted to know who had done it, and why.

The bad-something had made us feel horrible, all of us, because by then each of us had told someone what it was, until everyone knew.

Even our parents knew, because the principal had called each house. Our parents whispered while they drank their coffee, but when we came into the room, they went quiet.

Some of them hugged us at morning drop-off for way too long.

We missed the days
before the bad-something
appeared, because everything
was different now. Some of us
felt worried or confused or sad
or angry. No one felt nothing.

We were meaner
than we used to be.
Like when Devon went
to sharpen his pencil and
tripped, and we laughed.

Mrs. Martínez called the whole school to the gym.
To talk about "something important," she said.

Her voice crackled into the microphone as she told us that we were all special, that our school was special, and that she knew, more than anything else in the world, that we were kind, even if we forgot sometimes.

She told us the bad-something had no place here.

Then our teachers gave us all pins made from ribbons in our school colors. "To remember who we are," the principal said.

We held our heads a little bit higher when we walked back to our classrooms.

Mr. Gilbert sat in a circle with us.
His eyes were shiny when he said he
had a big project—an art project—
and we could all participate.

When the boys came into the girls'
bathroom, we snickered, but Mr. Gilbert
said it was okay, because we were all in
this together.

We painted and painted, straight through
recess, all over that bathroom wall.

Each one of us had something to add. Mateo drew flowers, and Rosa drew dragons, and Kai drew both, plus rainbows and dogs and lots of smiling people.

We drew our whole class. And then we kept going. We drew our whole school. The principal liked it so much she let us keep working on it, a little bit each day, until practically the whole wall was covered.

We couldn't believe
what we'd made!

But then we remembered.

We asked Mr. Gilbert if the bad-something was still there and he said yes, that somewhere deep underneath, it was still there. But we had changed it. We changed it when we covered that wall with our *good*-somethings.

an cloud

than gray

We studied our work and wrote poems about what we saw there. We wrote about how our painting had more green than gray, more sun than clouds. Then we wrote about the world outside the painting. We wrote about how there was more good than bad, more love than hate.

We are nicer than we used to be.

Devon reads his poem now, the very
first time he's read out loud in class.

Some kids smile and nod. Some kids lean
way forward so they won't miss a thing. Some
kids close their eyes and let his words wash over them.

We take our time to look at one another. We all
see something.

Something good.

AUTHOR'S NOTE

Something Good was inspired by real-life events at my children's schools. In one case, I knew what the "bad-something" was; in another, I never found out. I witnessed, as both a parent and classroom volunteer, the wide range of children's reactions to these troubling events, and I know that, just as there are varied reactions, there are also varied solutions. This book portrays just one way a school might deal with an incident of hate speech.

In my own life, I've found that creating art is a useful way to process strong emotions. At the end of this book, the children are kinder and more empathetic, but my hope is that the work doesn't stop there. Teaching children kindness in the classroom is absolutely vital, but it can only go so far, unless adults are willing to do the hard work of educating ourselves and advocating for programs and policies that respect and value all children.

If you're looking for a place to start, I've found Teaching Tolerance (tolerance.org) to be a tremendously useful source of information. For additional resources, I can also suggest Teaching for Change (teachingforchange.org) and EmbraceRace (embracerace.org). My hope is that, together, we can make more good-somethings happen in our homes, schools, and communities.

something good

WORDS BY MARCY CAMPBELL

PICTURES BY CORINNA LUYKEN

LITTLE, BROWN AND COMPANY
New York Boston

To all the good-somethings in my life,
especially Rick, Lily, and Whit
—MC

For my arts teachers—
Julia, Barbara, Andrea, Penny,
John, David, Rachel, and Dennis
—CL

ABOUT THIS BOOK

The illustrations for this book were done in gouache, colored pencil, and ink on paper. This book was edited by Andrea Spooner and designed by Saho Fujii. The production was supervised by Patricia Alvarado, and the production editor was Jen Graham. The text was set in Andrade Pro, and the display type is hand lettered.